It's OK to be Different

WRITTEN BY
SHARON PURTILL

ILLUSTRATED BY
SUJATA SAHA

It's OK to be Different

A Children's Picture Book About Diversity and Kindness

Revised Edition July 2020

Written by Sharon Purtill and illustrated by Sujata Saha

Published by Dunhill Clare Publishing - Ontario, Canada
Copyright © 2019 Dunhill Clare Publishing
dunhillclare@gmail.com

Hardcover edition   ISBN: 978-0-9734104-4-0
Paperback edition   ISBN: 978-0-9734104-5-7
Digital epub edition ISBN: 978-0-9734104-6-4
Digital mobi edition ISBN: 978-0-9734104-7-1

Library and Archives Canada Cataloguing in Publication

Other books by this author include:

Kids Say and Do the Darndest Things: A Journal for Recording
Each Surprising, Sweet, Crazy and Hilarious Moment
(Perfect for parents with little ones, and it's available in many fun colours)

It's OK to be Different

This book is dedicated to
every young child who is bold
enough to be themselves,
and appreciate the wonderful
diversity around them.

We are all different.

Do you know each and
every person is different?

It's true!

If everyone looked and
acted the same, how would
we know who was who?

Some kids love to swim

and some like to hike.

Some like to dance

and some love to bike.

We are all different.

Some kids love the colour blue
and some adore yellow.

Maybe pink is your favourite colour like this little fellow.

Some kids love to build towers out of blocks.

Some kids enjoy wearing
different coloured socks.

We are all different.

Some kids have blond hair and light coloured skin.

Some kids have dark hair and dark coloured skin.

Some kids are **big** and some kids are small.

Some kids are short

and others are tall!

We are all different.

Some kids are great at science
and math. Other kids choose
a whole 'nother path.

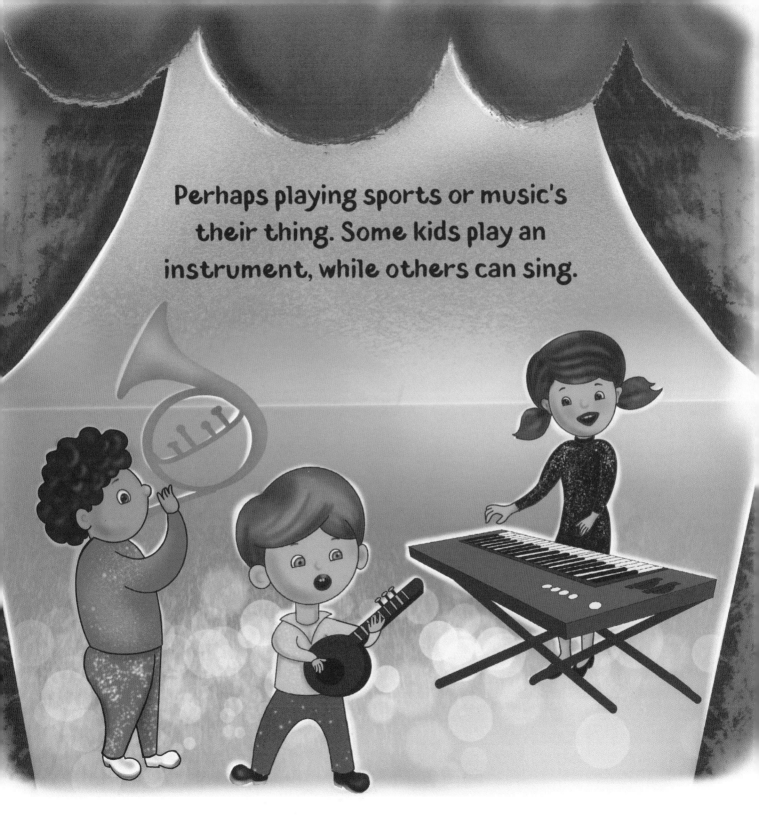

Perhaps playing sports or music's their thing. Some kids play an instrument, while others can sing.

We are all different.

Some kids wear glasses that help them to see. Some kids talk with an accent that's different from me.

Some kids get to ride in cool looking chairs.
They take the ramp while others take the stairs.

We are all different.

Some kids have glasses, crutches, wheelchairs and slings, but it's never OK to make fun of these things.

Even though we don't all

look, act or sound alike,

one thing is true.

Every child is an individual,

a person like YOU.

You should always
be KIND to
those who are
different from you.

Because to them, YOU are different too.

Remember, it's OK to be different.

It's OK to be YOU!

You were made to be different.

You were made to be ... YOU.

It's OK to be Different

Who do you know who is
different from you?

If you have noticed differences
maybe they have too.

What about them makes them
different from you?

And if you wanted to show them
kindness, what would you do?

Printed in Great Britain
by Amazon